THE MYSTERIOUS CHILD

WENDY ELMER

authorHOUSE®

AuthorHouse™
1663 Liberty Drive
Bloomington, IN 47403
www.authorhouse.com
Phone: 1-800-839-8640

Published by AuthorHouse   07/17/2012

ISBN: 978-1-4772-4415-9 (sc)
ISBN: 978-1-4772-4416-6 (e)

Library of Congress Control Number: 2012912637

C·H·A·P·T·E·R—1

Police officer Michael ryan was having a good day. He worked the night shift in Newark, New Jersey. He enjoyed the night shift because he got to spend time with his kids. It was the first day of summer and this was the first night he got to train a new recruit. He was at the ceremony when he was approached with this news. He spent half the day in the park and the other half sleeping.

At around 10:00 that night they were approached by a transvestite named Anna. Michael had to wran his partner first that they were talking to a man. His birth name was Michael.

Officer Ryan said: "Good evening Anna. How is business tonight?"

Anna laughed and said: "Business has been rather slow lately. The money I make from prostituting goes into my savings account for a total sex change. I wanted to talk to you because no matter what I look like or do you have always treated me with respect and dignity."

Officer Ryan blushed and said: "We try to my friend. By the way, weren't you a blonde last week?"

Anna laughed and said: "Yes. I switch off sometimes depending on my night. It is not true that blonds get more."

Officer Ryan asked: "What was it you wanted to ask me?"

Anna said: "If I see something out of place do I tell you about it or just ignore it?"

Officer Ryan said: "You tell us about it. Never worry about being wrong. That is what we get paid for. By the way, have you found out what hospital does that operation?"

Anna said: "No. I am on the internet searaching, but so far I haven't found one yet."

Officer Ryan said: "I can help you with that. The only hospital that does that is in Colorado. Start your search there. One more piece of advice Anna. Since you are putting money in a savings account if you put in more than a thousand dollars the bank is obligated to report it to the IRS for income. Stay under the radar by making deposits in small increments."

Anna said: "Thank you Ryan. I didn't know about that. One thing you should look out for is a strange child in the neighborhood. I have lived here all my life and she just looks like she is from elsewhere."

Ryan asked: "Did you speak to her?"

Anna said: "Yes. She said she was alone in the world. She said she was a ward of the state, but the state didn't take custody of her because there was nobody to make that phone call. She asked me where was the hospital. I directed her to Newark General."

Officer Ryan asked: "What did she look like?"

Anna said: "Blond hair, blue eyes. Buzz cut style."

Officer Ryan said: "Thank you Anna. My partner and I will drive over there and search the hospital. Why don't you come with us because you know what she looks like?"

Anna said: "Does this qualify as a Code Adam?"

Office Ryan said: "Maybe. We'll think about it on the way over." He told his partner to call in to dispatch where they will be. His partner forgot to use police codes. He spoke in full sentences and in proper grammar. When they got there Officer Ryan explained to the guard the situation. They guard said there were only two entrances open during the night. One was the emergency room and one was the main entrance. The main entrance was open just in case the family member dies and the family wanted to be there at the time of death. Everybody is instructed to stop by the security desk for okay. The nurse's desk is instructed to call security to let them up to visit. The security guard called up four colleagues and decided to call out a Code Adam after all. One was instructed to search all the stairwells from roof to basement. Another one went to the Emergency Room and checked the booths for treatment one at a time. He will never take a lead the same again. He had to puke after seeing some of the stuff. After a two hour extensive search everybody came up blank. No child had been found. Officer Ryan thanked security for their help and canceled the Code Adam. They drove Anna home for the evening. They drove back to the precinct and clocked out for the evening. Officer Ryan told his sergeant about the evening's events.

C·H·A·P·T·E·R—2

adrian was not looking forward to going to work today. He had been a tour guide at the Liberty Bell for ten years now. Everyday he had to do the same routine. Greet people on the buses and direct them to the Liberty Bell. This is the summer, so there are a lot more kids running around and screaming. Every year at least once a year a child got lost and they always had to drop everything and find them. Today was a little different though. He gathered the people around the Liberty Bell and there was a young child standing at the front. The group leaders looked at her questioningly. Once of them pulled Adrian aside and communicated that she wasn't with them.

Adrian had to go and get the supervisor. He explained the situation and tried to figure out what to do. When they returned to the Liberty Bell the child had vanished. The supervisor asked about the girl. They decided to make an announcement over the PA system. The announcement said: "Attention all tourists. We are looking for a child that

might have been separated from her group. She is about 4'
6" tall and weighs about 50 lbs. You are not in trouble, but
we just want to reunite you with whomever you belong to.
Somebody must have paid your admission fees to the park.
We normally don't sell tickets to unsupervised under age
children. If this child is out there or if you know where she
is please direct her to the nearest first aid station. That would
be the green building with the red cross symbol outside. At
the end of the day the child never materialized. Everybody
just dismissed the case as an odd situation. Security was
reminded about the rules of selling tickets to minors. They
were also reminded not to allow into the park children alone
without being accompanied by a parent or group. Adrian
thought maybe she joined the end of the line of a group. She
was so small it was easy not to notice her.

C-H·A·P·T·E·R—3

George Mueller was a thirteen year old Amish boy who lived in Ohio. His mother promised to bake him his favorite cake. A vanilla cake with vanilla icing. A blue sugar flower on top and blue piping icing all around the top. His mother sent him out to the barn with his father to work with the horses. She also wanted to get him away from her so she can get to baking the cake.

George's father promised him to teach him to drive the horse and buggy. When he turned twelve years old his father told him to take care of the horses for one year. He shocked the family by succeeding in this chore. He never gave up or complained about mucking out the stalls. Learning to drive the buggy was a right of passage for an Amish child. To hook up the buggy is called hitching up the team. The back was very heavy to pick up and move outside. The horses were the easy part. They were trained to move on command. It took 20 minutes for him to do it the first time. George senior said the horses thought it was play time and they were fooling around with junior. He had to give a command to get to work. Finally they were ready to move. They climbed in and his father took the reins. You pull the left one to go and the right one to stop. He had to pull hard because the reins were connected to the horse's head. He had to hold the reins in one hand. They got onto the public road and stopped the wagon. Junior asked: "Why did we stop poppa?" Poppa said: "Junior, look at that kid up ahead. Have you ever seen her before?"

Junior looked into the rear view mirror and said: "No sir. Maybe she lives in the city down the road."

Poppa said: We are too far from the city. A child that young should not be traveling alone. Look. She is staring at the horse." He looked at the girl and said: "Hi there little lady. What brings you out to the country?"

The girl said: "Nowhere special. I am alone in the world. Legally I am a ward of the state, but the state never took custody of me. Nobody called the state to tell them."

Poppa asked: "You are a ward of what state?"

The girl said: "Of the United States."

Poppa asked: "Would you like to come to our house for a birthday party for my son?"

The girl said: "Oh yes please. Can I play with the horses?"

Poppa said: "Yes. Now climb up there and stay seated" Poppa took the reins and showed them how to make a left hand turn with the horses. When they got back to the house dad instructed junior to unhitch the team and return the horses to the stalls. The two kids ran off and played with the animals. When dad entered the house he said: "Honey, don't get mad."

His wife looked up and said: "What did you do or what did junior do?"

Dad said: "I did something strange. I picked up a hitchhiker and brought her home to play with the animals."

Mom asked: "How old is this person?"

Dad said: "She looks like she is about seven years old or so. She claims to be a ward of the state, but the state never took custody of her."

Mom asked: "What is her name?"

Dad said: "She claims her name is Martha Washington. I don't know what to think of that name. I have no proof either way whether or not she is lying."

Mom said: "Maybe we should call the police?"

Dad said: "We don't have a phone. We are isolated out here from society. Even if I managed to get word to a cop it would take at least 24 hours to get some advice or answers. We have no electricity, so by the time the cops get here it would be dark. We would only see them in shadow. Our religion tells us to the Christian and open hearted to strangers. I took her off the road and now she can at least have a bath and a good hot mean in her stomach." The kids were called in to have the party. Mom said first comes lunch, then the cake. Lunch consisted of Fried chicken, mashed potatoes and string beans. Martha ate a lot of food. She has no pockets, so she couldn't save it for later or tomorrow. She had eaten seconds on the string beans. Mom just kept feeding her as much as she wanted. Finally it came time for the cake. She made 5 roses on it this time. One rose for each person. After dinner and cake mom told the kids it was bath time. Martha said that she wanted to go in first. She scrubbed herself raw. Mom came in to help her wash her hair. She ran her fingers through her hair looking for bugs or lice or something. She found nothing. She went straight to bed after her bath. While she slept mom washed her clothes. Unfortunately when everybody got up in the morning Martha was gone.

Junior asked: "Poppa, what do we do now?"

Poppa said: "Now all we can do is pray that God keeps her safe. We did what we could for her. Eventually she has to be reunited with her own family. We fulfilled our obligations by taking her in. One more thing Junior. I went to the outhouse around 2:00 this morning. Coming back to the house I noticed our neighbor next door coming back from his outhouse. I asked him if he saw a strange child and he said yes he saw one walking westward."

CHAPTER 4

Two professors were on the lawn of Indiana State University having a picnic lunch. They had just started the summer semester and were discussing their experiences with their classes. Fred was a psychology teacher who taught mainly Introduction to Psychology. He looked up and saw what looked like a spirit of a 7 year old girl. His friend Milo said he looked like he saw a ghost. Milo almost wanted to pick him up and carry him to the infirmary.

Fred asked; "Milo, do you see a 7 year old girl staring at us?"

Milo said: "Yes I do. What is your name little girl?"

The girl said: "Hi. My name is Tiffany."

Milo asked: "What are you doing on a college campus?"

Tiffany said: "I walked past the guard and here I am."

Fred asked: "Where do you live?"

Tiffany said: "I am a nomad. I don't stay too long anywhere."

Fred asked: "At your age how do you know the word nomad?"

Tiffany said: "I spend a lot of time in public libraries. The first book I look at is a dictionary."

Milo asked: "Where do you sleep at night when you get to a new place?"

Tiffany said: "I spent one winter in a boiler room in a church. The Catholic Churches are the easiest places to hid. I even spent a little bit of time in a confessional. That was fun. For some reason the light didn't go on."

Milo asked: "How do you manage to shower?"

Tiffany said: "That's easy. I snick into the bathroom of the pediatrics wing and found that it had a visitor's shower. I just helped myself. Most people are respectful and don't barge in."

Milo asked: "Would you like to come to my house tonight so you can have a warm bed?"

Tiffany said: "Oh yes please. I would like that very much." They left the campus together. When they got o Milo's house his wife was surprised at this unexpected guest. His wife's name was Margaret. After Tiffany went to bed that night Margaret asked Milo where she came from.

Milo said "I don't really know where she came from. She seemed to appear out of nowhere. I thought she was a spirit. At 11:00 that night Milo got a phone call that Fred had a heart attack a few hours ago. He was in the hospital, but was not expected to pull through. Milo turned sheet white and couldn't stand up. When he got up in the morning Fred had passed away in his sleep. He never felt anything. Margaret wanted to call the police but she went to check on Tiffany instead. She was gone just as suddenly as she appeared.

C-H·a·P-T·e·R—5

It was the day after Black Friday in Bloomington, Minnesota. All the guards were plumb out exhausted from the day before. Three people actually had to take the day off to sleep. They had to deal with the usual stupidity from humanity. They had your average drunk creting a disturbance at the food court. When they finished wrestling him to the ground he admitted to loading his pants. Then they had a diabetic who fainted in the theater line. All the guards were trained in medical aid just for such emergencies. It took an army of security to pull off an EMS arrival and not get lost. Every guard was assigned a certain section to look after. This way nobody had to wait too long for them.

Simon Tray was anther guard on another floor. He had to deal with a teenage shoplifter in one of the stores. It was a high end Gucci store. The manager wanted to press charges and arrest the girls. Simon allowed the teenagers to call their parents. He advised the parents to meet the girls down at the station house. Before he called the cops they were taken down to the basement in the freight elevator and had their pictures taken and fingerprints taken. Then the state police came and took over. They were given a court date and were found guilty. They got probation.

John Dooley was assigned to watch the TV's for the day. It was his job t watch for signals from the merchants that help was needed. About an hour into his day he noticed someone walking in appealingly alone. It was a little blond haired girl. The guard at the door stopped a few people to ask if she was with them. She was seen heading towards the restroom. John made an announcement on his walkie talkie to follow the child around but don't harm her or scare her. The manager of Arbies head the announcement on the guard's walkie talkie. It was brought to his attention because people are more likely to eat before shop. He spotted her and alerted the cameras. Four guards came running towards Arbies and they all stopped short. The manager of Arbies came out from the kitchen and said: "Hi there little lady."

The girl said: "Hi."

The manager asked: "What is your name?"

The girl said: "Michelle, what about you?"

The manager said: "My name is Mark. By the way, where are your escorts?"

Michelle said: "I don't need escorts."

Mark asked: "What store did you come to?"

Michelle said: "I like the bookstores."

Mark asked: "Are you hungry?"

Michelle said: "Yes. I guess I could use a little something to eat."

Mark ordered a number three special. A chicken fingers and French fries with a soda. When she sat down to eat Mark said: "Can I see the bottom of your shoes please?"

Michelle took her shoes off and showed them to Mark.

Mark said: "Thank you. I'll tell you what I can do for you. Let me buy you a new pair of sneakers and you can go on your way."

Michelle seemed okay with that. She finished her lunch and said: "Mark, I am finished."

Mark said: "Okay Michelle. Let's spend the day together. First I will take you to our resident podiatrist and make sure your feet are in good shape. The podiatrist cut her toe nails and made sure she didn't have any infections. Miraculously there weren't any problems with her feet. He gave her a free pair of slipper sox. Next was the stride rite shoe store. Her foot was measured and she was found to wear a size 3 child's foot. When they finished in the shoe store Mark offered to buy her a coat and hat and gloves and scarf. The weather in the dead of winter can get very brutal in Minnesota. Mark forgot to ask her about her coat and hat. That information was radioed from John during the course of the day. Michelle thanked Mark for spending time with her and helping her out. She left the mall and was never seen again out there. The next morning John called the state police and alerted them to the child being seen unsupervised. The cops told him he should have called yesterday. Mark said she never mentioned where she was from or where her parents were. During the day Mark sent hand signals to John through the cameras to signal where they were and what they were up to next.

C-H·A·P-T-E·R—6

It was a beautiful spring day in Sparta, Illinois a few months later. It was the first day that everybody was outside without a jacket. Michelle was approached by a young man who looked like a construction worker. He had long hair and was not very attractive. He saw Michelle sitting on a bench across the street from an Irish Pub. She didn't really know what a pub was. She didn't try to move and just looked at the man. His name was Phillip Naughton. He smiled at her and said: "Good morning there. What is your name?"

She answered and said: "My name is Gabriella. People call me Gabby for short. They say I talk too much, but I don't believe them."

Phillip asked: "Are you new in town? I have never seen you before."

Gabby said: "I am new in town. Legally I am a ward of the state, but the state never took custody of me because nobody called them to tell them."

Phillip asked: "You are a ward of what state?"

Gabby said: "Of the United States."

Phillip asked: "How long have you been a ward of the United States?"

Gabby said: "I am not sure. I am a nomad."

Phillip asked: "Where did you learn that word nomad?"

Gabby said: "I read a dictionary. I hang out in libraries."

Phillip asked: "How do you bathe without a home?"

Gabby said: "I hang out in the pediatrics ward of hospitals. In the bathrooms they always have a visitor's shower. People seem to be very respectful of privacy."

Phillip asked: "How do you manage to eat?"

Gabby said: "I have to steal a lot of fruit. I am not proud of that, but sometimes you have to do things you are not proud of."

Phillip asked: "Are you hungry now?"

Gabby said: "Yes sir. I could probably use a bathroom too."

Phillip asked: "How old are you exactly?"

Gabby said: "I am not sure exactly. I have been on my own for so long I lost track. Want to hear what trick I pulled?"

Phillip said: "Sure. I am always looking for new tricks to pull on my kids."

Gabby said: "I was wandering around a hospital. There was a woman who convinced me to take her place for surgery. She gave me her wristband and hospital johnny. I climbed into bed and she got dressed and took off. Two orderlies came in and gave me an IV line. Then the next thing I knew they whisked me off to surgery. I was a little bit asleep by the time I woke up something was different about me. I thought it was the anesthesia. I had a warm bed and good food for a week. I also had a shower every night."

Phillip asked: "What state did this happen in?"

Gabby said: "I don't remember exactly."

Phillip said: "That sounds scary. Where did they operate on you?"

Gabby said: "I am not sure, but I didn't have any stiches anywhere."

Phillip said: "Let's go across the street to the pub where you can wash up and eat something."

Gabby said: "Oh thank you sir!! Please hold my hand." They walked across to the pub. When they entered they met the bartender named Irene.

Phillip said: "Good afternoon Irene. This is my new friend Gabby. I brought her in here to have your famous hamburger deluxes."

Irene said: "Oh wonderful Phillip. Gabby, the bathroom is over there on the right. Phillip, why don't you help me in the kitchen."

When they got in there Phillip started to explain how he came to meet Gabby. When he finished his tale Irene suggested they call the police and say it is a possible sighting of a missing child.

Sergeant Buxley answered the phone on the second ring. Phillip went through his tale again.

Sergeant Buxley said: "Meet me outside the pub. We will go in together as long lost buddies. Phillip did as he was told. Gabby came out of the restroom and approached the bar. She asked where Phillip was. Irene said that he was just outside waiting for someone. She sat down and got down to the business of eating. She asked for a Coke to drink with it. Phillip meanwhile was met outside by Sergeant Buxley. They went over the story a second time. Finally Sergeant Buxley said this sounds like a missing child case. After all she didn't just all off the face of the earth. She didn't fall from the sky either. He took off his police shirt and the other thing he put on was just a sweatshirt. He didn't want to scare her off. They entered and found gabby in the pub eating her food and drinking her Coke. Phillip said: "This is my friend Joseph. We haven't seen each other lately so we decided to get together today. Irene said: "Eat your food boys. Everything is getting cold." Joseph put his napkin in his neck and started eating.

Joseph said: "So Gabby, where are you from originally?"

Gabby said: "I have been alone for so long I don't remember anymore."

Joseph asked: "How long have you been alone?"

Gabby said: "I don't know. I have always had a fascination with the state of Nevada. I always wanted to see the Mojave desert. I tried to walk west, but sometimes I get turned around and go north or south for a while. If I see a bus stop sometimes I will hop a bus and take it to the last stop. That saves me from foot aches. Are there any living people in the Mojave Desert?"

Joseph said: "Yes. There is a town called Laughlin. The Mojave Desert goes as far as California."

Gabby said: "I read somewhere that the U.S. Army has a nuclear plant out there."

Joseph said: "I know what you mean. It is all fenced in and guarded. You can't get in there without being stopped at the gate."

Phillip said: "To be honest with you they wouldn't let in Jesus Christ Himself if he walked up to the gate."

Irene said: "Wash your mouth out with soap for that blasphemous remark!"

Phillip said: "Sorry dear. I will go to confession tomorrow."

Joseph said: "I'll take your glass you are drinking out of. We need it for the precinct." He took it without another word from either of them. Gabby excused herself and went to the restroom. After about fifteen minutes Irene went into the restroom and discovered she was gone. The three of them searched the pub up and down and she just vanished into thin air. Joseph took the glass to the precinct anyway. Joseph said: "Well Phillip, at least you did a Corporal Work of Mercy today. You fed the hungry and you gave shelter to the homeless. This was one hour she wasn't out in the street facing danger. A few weeks later Phillip was back in the pub eating lunch. Joseph entered and asked: "Have you heard from that little girl that was here a few weeks ago?"

Irene said: "No. We never saw her again."

Joseph said: "Too bad. We got a hit off the glass. That is a missing child from New York. I informed them of her appearance and I updated her picture. Their picture shows her with long blonde hair. Her eyes are the same. Her facial features are pretty much the same too.

C·H·A·P·T·E·R—7

It was Christmas time in Branson, Missouri. There were tourists all over the place. Branson was a very popular town because everybody in town got together and put Christmas together. They constructed the North Pole for Santa to sit in. Some people dressed the horses and some drove the visitors from the hotels to the North Pole. Some even did the hay rides. They also had to drive them back down the mountain when they finished. There was a carnival like atmosphere on the top of the mountain. It was isolated from the major cities in the south. All of this was done on a volunteer basis. Nobody got paid for their work. Most of the volunteers were unemployed anyway, so they had plenty of time on their hands. The kids loved the hay rides. It looked better at night with the Christmas lights all lit up.

On this particular night there was a little girl who was waiting for a hayride. She seemed to be traveling alone. The driver noticed and asked the next person if she was with them. The driver was technologically in the know. He took her picture with his cell phone and e-mailed it to everybody in his address book. Everybody had the same response that nobody knew her. He started up the horses and off they rolled up the mountain. When they got there everybody dispersed. The driver alerted Santa Clause, who happened to bed the town sheriff. By the time they reached the top of the mountain every adult saw her picture and came up with a plan to take her in to safety. They were met by Mrs. Clause at the top. While they were talking at the front the little girl slipped away again unnoted. She wandered into the casino. The guard let her in and e-mailed everybody in her address book that she was safe and inside. The TV cameras weren't going to let her out of their sight. She didn't notice because it was on an old fashioned cat walk with the black covering on the ceiling. Even with all this security they still managed to lose her. They prayed that she was in the bathroom. There were no cameras inside the stalls. Especially the ladies room. Nobody wanted to lose their lunch on the job. The elves that scattered around the casino were undercover cops. Mrs. Clause found our little guest coming out of the stall. She said: "Good evening my friend. What is your name?"

The girl answered: "My name is Daphne."

Mrs. Clause asked: "Are you visiting from out of town?"

Daphne answered: "Yes. I am a ward of the state, but the state never took custody of me. Nobody called the state to tell them."

Mrs. Clause asked; "You are a ward of what state?"

Daphne said: "I am a ward of the United States."

Mrs. Clause asked: "What happened to your parents?"

Daphne said: "I don't remember. I just woke up and they were gone. I just started walking west. I want to go to Nevada. I want to see the Mojave Desert and touch the cacti."

Mrs. Clause asked: "How long have you been wandering the United States?"

Daphne said: "I don't remember. I rely on the kindness of strangers. People open up their homes to me so I can shower and they give me a hot meal. Then I move on."

Mrs. Clause asked: "How do you spend your days?"

Daphne said: "I spend my days in libraries reading. I am small, so I just curl up in a corner less traveled. Nobody notices me because I usually sneak past behind them unnoticed. Now I have a question for you. I noticed the airplanes are flying very low. Is there an airport nearby?"

Mrs. Clause said: "Yes. About a mile north of here."

One thing Daphne didn't know was that their conversation was recorded by a mini tape recorder on the wrist watch. Mrs. Clause found Santa and handed over the tape. They sent it off to New York along with the video tape and once again it was confirmed that they were talking to a missing child. The tape was played for Daphne's aunt and uncle. They confirmed the sound of the voice. They also recognized her face. The New York cops assured the family that every cop worldwide would be notified and on the lookout for her. All that was left was to be thankful people reach out to help her. She is obviously a brilliant youngster to have survived these long winter months. Her aunt and uncle thanked the cops for not giving up on their case.

CHAPTER—8

Daphne made it to the airport. She sat down on the radiators and watched the people rushing to and fro catching planes and cabs. Security cameras picked up her image and they sent out a red alert to be on the lookout. An underage child traveling alone is supposed to raise red flags. After Daphne rested a while she started to stake out the security points. She noticed at 3:00 in the afternoon that the lines were getting long for the early evening flights. She snuck right through the metal detectors unnoticed nad sashed right onto a plane. She noticed the food was being delivered and everybody was busy in the kitchen. She fell asleep in the bathroom. By the time she woke up they had taken off the ground. The shaking of the turbulence woke her up. She didn't realize it at the time but she was on an Aer Lingus plane on her way to Dublin, Ireland. A stewardess knocked on the door and asked if she was all right. She said she was fine, just fell asleep on the toilet. The stewardess escorted her back to her seat and she settled in for the night's flight. Dinner was served shortly after. It was a heavenly meal of potatoes, beef and carrots and peas. After she ate she wrapped the blanket around herself and settled in for the night. When they landed the pilot announced that they have landed. He said: "Welcome to Ireland. The weather is clear and in the 60's. On the way out people were saying thank you to the pilot for a smoothe landing. As Daphne passed them the pilot asked the stewardess who was that little girl. Irene said she fell asleep in the bathroom and she escorted her back to her seat.

The pilot asked: "Where are her parents?"

Irene said: "Come to think of it I don't know. I was so anxious to free up the bathroom I think I forgot to ask."

The pilot picked up the phone and notified Immigration and Naturalization desk to be on the lookout for this child. She read all the signs and waltzed right through. The difference this time was that she was stopped at the other side. She was half way toward the luggage claim when she felt a hand on each shoulder. They turned her around and marched her right into the office. She was sat into the chair with two immigration officers facing her on the other side of the desk. The sergeant's name was Jack. He was the speaker of the group.

Jack asked: "What is your name?"

The girl answered: "My name is Mildred."

Jack asked: "Where were you born?"

Mildred answered: "I was born in the United States. I am alone in the world. I have always had a dream to walk in the footsteps of my grandmother. She was born in County Cork. I wanted to move to Ireland because I wanted to walk in my grandmother's footsteps. I have nobody in America. I don't know if I have anybody in Ireland either. I am alone in the world no matter where I live."

Jack asked: "Do you have a passport?"

Mildred said: "I don't know what that is. I never intended to be trouble, but I am just trying to survive."

Jack asked: "How long specifically have you been alone in the world?"

Mildred said: "I am not sure. I lost track of time."

Jack asked: What state do you live in?"

Mildred said: "I have been wandering the United States."

Jack asked: "When did you last go to school?"

Mildred said: "I have never gone to school. I just read in libraries. My goal was to walk to the Mojave Desert. I have an interest in moving to the state of Nevada. I was hanging out in the airport and I went to the bathroom. I fell asleep on the toilet. When I woke up we were already in the air. It was a pure coincidence that I ended up here in Ireland.

The two officers excused themselves and a third one came in to make sure she doesn't slip away. She stood right in front of the door with her arms crossed. She could see the wires in Mildred's brain working overtime. For a woman cop she was awfully imposing. For the first time Mildred didn't move.

Jack asked: "So what do you think of that story?"

His partner Ethan said: "I think there are holes in that story."

Jack asked: "Where do you see the holes?"

Ethan said: "I don't buy that she picked the one plane

going to Ireland. Every airport has bathrooms all over the place. Why should she pick out an airplane coming here to go to the bathroom."

Jack said: "That doesn't sound very Christian of you. You sound like you don't believe she went to the bathroom."

Ethan said: "I believe we have an illegal alien on our hands. How did she manage to sneak past security? I think she staked out the airport and found holes in the system."

Jack asked: "What should we do with her?"

Ethan said: "Send her back wherever she came from."

Jack said: "The next returning flight leaves tomorrow morning for Chicago. For now the best thing we can do is put her up in the office. Now we have to feed her and give her a warm bed." They returned to the office and Ethan and Jack reentered. Jack was the spokesperson. He said: "So Mildred. It seems we have a situation here. This is considered a foreign country even though we speak English. In order to enter here you need a passport that says United States of America. It is a blue booklet. Since you have no family here we cannot allow you to enter. You need to go home and your foster family can apply for you. You are a minor. Legally we cannot have people wandering the streets unsupervised. Do you have money?"

Mildred said: "I have never needed money. People just feed me and give me shelter."

Jack said: "Over here we use shillings. We don't use the word dollars and cents. We cannot give money away for free. That would be against the rules. By the way Mildred. Have you ever been examined by a doctor?"

Mildred said: "Yes. I took the place of a patient and she

gave me her name bracelet. She got dressed and I got into bed. Then somebody brought me to another room and I went to sleep. When I woke up I looked for stitches but I didn't find any. I don't know what surgery they did."

Ethan asked: "Did anybody notice that your name bracelet was broken?"

Mildred said: "Yes. But they didn't bother to reattach it. I had a warm bed and three square meals for a week."

Ethan said: "For tonight you will need to stay here in our warm bunk bed and covers. You can crawl in. We will feed you a hot meal. Come with me. I will show you."

The next morning she was woken up and taken to an airplane. The stewardess directed her to her seat where she was told to stay where she was until they landed. The gentleman sitting next to her was an undercover immigration officer. His job was to make sure she didn't leave the plane for any reason. The plane landed in Chicago, Illinois. Once again she slipped right past immigration. She was alone again back in America. She switched to survival mode.

C·H·A·P·T·E·R—9

Mildred got off the plane and went to the bathroom again. She came out and looked around. She found an unguarded sign that said do not enter. She entered and found herself in the boarding area. She spent the night in a Catholic Cathedral right near the airport. She slipped in the exit door with a group coming out. She fell asleep in the confessional. By slipping in the exit door she avoided the metal detectors and scrutiny of the officers at the door. She got in and got hungry after a while. When she saw that the church was closed she went over to the tabernacle and ate all of the Communion Hosts. She was feasting on them when the door to the confessional burst open and she got caught once again. The priest's name was Father James McKenna. He said: "What are you doing here?"

Mildred said: "I got hungry, so I ate this stuff."

Father James asked: "What is your name?"

The girl answered: "My name is Anna."

Father James asked: "Where are your parents?"

Anna said: "They aren't here. They are Protestant."

Father James asked: "Did they leave you unsupervised?"

Anna said: "Yes. They went on a trip for the day."

Father James asked: "Where did they go for the day?"

Anna said: "They went to gamble in the casino somewhere."

Father James asked: "Which casino did they go to?"

Anna said: "I don't know. They got on a bus this morning."

Father James asked: "Are you hungry?"

Anna said: "Yes sir. Those round things I was eating didn't fill me up at all. It was like eating air."

Father James said: "You were lucky they weren't blessed yet." They walked back to the rectory together where they went to the kitchen. Father James asked the cook Mary-Ann to get Anna something to drink. He said: "Mary-Ann, please get Anna a drink and then come into my office for some talk. I want to go over next week's schedule with you."

Mary-Ann said: "Yes sir. I will be right there." Mary-Ann gave her some toast and said to make herself comfortable. She entered the office and Father James motioned for her to sit down. She said: "So Father James. Who is your little friend out there?"

Father James said: "I caught her eating all of the Communion Hosts from the tabernacle. She said it was like eating air. What is the nearest Protestant Church?"

Mary Ann said: "It is Church of the Holy Sepulchur.

Father James asked: "What is their phone number?"

Mary-Ann said: "I don't know their phone number."

He looked it up in the yellow pages and the reverant answered on the first ring. That always creeped him out when people did that.

Reverend Ike said: "Hello?"

Father James said: "Good morning reverend Ike. My name is Father James. I am the pastor of St. Peter's Cathedral."

Reverend Ike said: "Oh yes sir. We have met before. What can I do for you?"

Father James said: " We have a very peculiar situation over here. Did you happen to have a bus trip to the casino this morning?"

Reverend Ike said: "No sir. We have never gone to the casino."

Father James said: "We have a little girl here who gave us a tall tale about her parents going on a trip to the casino and leaving her alone for the day."

Reverend Ike asked: "Where did you meet this child?"

Father James said: "I caught her eating the Communion Hosts in the confessional. I have never seen her before."

Reverend Ike said: "I think I can help you unscramble this. I have a connection that can help us figure out who she is. May I come over and work this out with you?"

Father James said: "Gladly. There has to be somebody out there looking for this child."

Thirty minutes later Reverend Ike rang the doorbell. He was standing there with a friend of his Jacob McGeevey. Jacob was an undercover police officer. He made a plan to feed her something the she needs a fork to eat with. Mary-Ann made her French Fries. It took 8 minutes in the microwave. She started to eat with her fingers, but Father James told her to use a fork. At the end of the meal she realized nobody else was eating. Jacob said they were waiting for toast. Mary-Ann realized she forgot to put it on. Father James brought her upstairs to bed for the evening. They adjourned for the evening and Jacob took with him the fork she used. He was careful not to touch it too much. He didn't want his fingerprints to smudge her fingerprints. At 11:00 that night Father James got a phone call that she was a missing child from New York. He faxed the picture to the New York cops to update their files. Father James promised to bring her to the precinct first thing in the morning to be reunited with her family. Father James asked: "When did you take her picture?"

Jacob said: "I took it with my cell phone. There wasn't any flash needed. Through the magic of technology the tech geeks were able to upload a picture from the cell phone to the main frame computer. Jacob wouldn't even try to figure out how it was done. Unfortunately in the morning Anna was gone. Once again she gave everybody the slip. She seemed to slip off the face of the earth. Reverend Ike and Father James prayed that God would watch over her and keep her safe until her family can be reunited with her.

CHAPTER—10

Once again Anna found herself at an airport reading he departures board. She found a flight of interest. She snuck through the metal detectors and sashed through to the right gate. She waltzed onto the plane and went into the bathroom. She fell asleep again and woke up after the plane took off. This time she landed in Juneau, Alaska. She knew that was the biggest small town in America. It was also the smallest airport she had ever seen. She found a saloon and a cruise ship. She always wanted to sail on a ship. Her first plan was to grab something to eat. She walked into the saloon and found a lot of advertisements about buying gold bars and going into a cave to dig for gold. The diggers were supposed to bring their nuggets back to the saloon and get paid for them. The saloon came to a dead stop when she walked in. The bar tender's name was Marge. She asked: "Hey kid. Where are you from?"

Anna said: "I am from down state."

Marge asked: "What is your name?"

Anna said: "My name is Kim."

Marge asked: "How old are you?"

Kim said: "I am ten years old."

Marge asked: "Where are your parents?"

Kim said: "We are visiting Alaska on the cruise ship. They are on the ship gambling. I was told to go out and explore Alaska."

Marge asked: "Where is your boarding pass to get back on the ship?"

Kim searched her pockets but couldn't come up with anything. She said: "I guess I left it on the ship."

Marge asked: "How do you plan on getting back on the ship without that ID card?"

Kim said: "With my good looks. I guess I will smile and look adorable." The guy sitting next to her was an under cover police officer. He took her picture with his cell phone and e-mailed it to the captain of the ship. He responded about fifteen minutes later and said that this child was not a passenger on that cruise ship. He then e-mailed the picture to his captain back at the precinct. He was told to bring the child in and he would reunite her with her aunt and uncle whom have been looking for her for over two years. Kim went to the bathroom and was never seen again in Juneau, Alaska. She gave everybody the slip. She ended up back in the airport. Her next plane ride was to Detroit Michigan. She had never been there before. She was excited to see someplace new. She was getting used to flying. The angels above made sure it was a smooth flight every time she snuck onto a plane. Kim was resourceful and found a way to sneak on the the Carnival Cruise Line boat. She simply found another gangway that was unguarded. Because of the weather conditions the boat was rerouted to Detroit, Michigan. That was the best week of her life. She had an unending supply of food. She managed to sleep in stairwells and a few times she went into the state rooms. Luckily she was never caught. She had a story in her head at the ready just in case she was questioned. While she was asleep one night the captain put her hand on a machine that was portable. It was a no match found. The captain put the word out not to bother her. Everybody knew at that point that she was a stowaway. He notified the Detroit Police Department of his situation. He was advised to leave her alone and there would be undercover police officers to meet the boat. Kim was so tired she slept right through the hand scanner. The boat pulled into the slot and the undercover officer was right there. The captain was there and he brought him into his office to show him the picture he took of the child. He was instructed to let the passengers off and he would take custody of the child. It didn't work out that way. The child never appeared. The ship was cleared and the search was underway. Every inch was searched but she didn't appear in any stairwell or stateroom. Sixteen hours later the search was called off.

C-H·A·P·T·E·R—11

After Kim exited the boat she found herself wandering around again. It took her a while to figure out what she was going to do. She knew it would come to her eventually. Jeb McDonnell and his partner Sharon Newton were two of the first Animal Cops in the city of Detroit. Their job was to investigate animal abandonment and animal abuse cases. Jeb had been on the job for at least ten years. Sharon had been with him for six years. They seemed to be a perfect match together. They had a call about some abandoned dogs an abandoned house. They arrived and found the front door open. They entered and found Kim sitting on the floor by the fireplace. She said: "Hi there. Is it still raining?"

Jeb said: "No. It stopped. What is your name?"

Kim said: "My name is Cher."

Jeb asked: "Where do you live?"

Cher said: "I am alone in the world. I have no home to call my own. Are you here about the doggies?"

Jeb said: "Yes. I am here to check on them."

Cher said: "They are two Doberman Pinchers. They came outside and led me in here last night."

Sharon asked; "Did anybody leave towels behind so you can dry off?"

Cher said: "No. It wasn't raining yet when they led me inside."

Sharon asked: "Who let the dogs out?"

Cher said: "I let them out. They just never came back in. They never barked our scratched at the door. Jeb excused himself and went out to the backyard. He found the dogs shaking from being wet and sneezing themselves silly. His first call was to Sharon.

Jeb said: "Hi Sharon. I see the dogs."

Sharon said: "Are you kidding me?"

Jeb said: "No. I got a look at the dogs. I think they bother have colds. I have to call the office and see if they can advise us on what to do with the child."

Sharon said: "Fine. Call me back when you know something."

Cher said: "When I woke up this morning it had already stopped raining. I didn't think to let the dogs in. I was half asleep when I vaguely heard the rain. I assumed the dogs would run next door or into the dog house."

Sharon said: "Don't worry about it. They are yapping away out there and sound very happy. Jeb in the meantime called his boss Mark on the phone outside. He said: "Mark, we are at the abandoned house. We have a rather unusual situation over here. We found the dogs, but we may have found a missing child. What should we do about her?"

Mark said: "Good God Jeb!!! What have you stumbled

into? I'll tell you what. Bring the dogs in and the child. I will call Detroit cops and get them over here. How old would you say she is?"

Jeb said: "Maybe about ten years old. She said she was alone in the world. I don't know if I believe that or not."

Mark said: "Bring all of them in, but give me five minutes to do this."

Jeb said; "Yes sir." Jeb hung up and called his partner Sharon. He told her what to do. Sharon told Cher: "How would you like to come with us?"

Cher said: "Where? Can we bring the doggies?"

Sharon said: "Yes. You can play with them for a while. Sharon opened the door and the dogs bolted into the house. They really took a shining to Cher. They knocked her down and started romping and running all over her. Sharon and Jeb stood back and watched the show for five minutes. Cher felt good when she finished all that giggling.

She had no fear of the dogs. Jeb and Sharon both knew it was going to be an easy adoption of these characters. They loaded themselves into the car. They broke the rules slightly by allowing the dogs to ride in the back seat instead of in the cages.

Mark in the meantime called Detroit plice and requested two uniformed police officers to come to the DSPCA. She explained the situation and was told they would be right there. Mark said:" I don't mean to be rude, but could I ask you to bring 6 orders from McDonalds? We might gain the child's trust by feeding her."

The officer laughed and said; "No problem sir. Please meet us outside the adoptions door and my two best officers can talk to you then."

Unfortunately the two police officers got there after Jeb and Sharon. When Jeb and Sharon drove up Mark said: "Hello little lady. Sharon here will show you to the playroom we have set up for the dogs. We will leave you three in there to play for a while. Some people are coming and bringing McDonalds lunch. Sharon will come and get you then. The three of them ran down the hall. Myrtle was another employee sitting behind a one way glass observing the behavior of dogs. She made sure Cher wasn't injured. As soon as they got into the playroom one of the dogs found a ball and gave it to Cher to throw. It was hard to tell who was having more fun. Sharon excused herself and reported to Mark's office. They sat around the table and explained the situation to the officers. Sharon went to the playroom and got Cher. They went to the office and sat down to eat Chicken McNuggets and French Fries. They got a Coke to drink with their meal. Cher ate fast and was satisfied when she was finished.

Officer Jacob said: "So Cher. Tell us about yourself. Where are you from originally?

Cher said: "I have been alone in the world for most of my life. I have a fascination wit the Mojave Desert. I am trying to get to Las Vegas. It would be easy to hide in a crowd."

Officer Jacob asked: "How do you eat?"

Cher said: "I rely on the kindness of strangers. I travel by foot, plane, and boat. I just came back from Alaska. Usually I just go to the bathroom and fall asleep. When I wake up we are already in the air."

Officer Jacob asked: "What was your favorite made of transportation?"

Cher said: "That's easy. My favorite was the cruise ship. I was in Juneau, Alaska and snuck onto the ship. I had unlimited access to food and sleep. There is a code of traveling in an airport."

Officer Jacob asked: "What code would that be?"

Cher said: "No matter how much security you think there is there is always at least one that is unguarded. I am small and wiry, so it is easy to sneak right past security unseen."

Officer Jacob asked: "How did you come about on a cruise ship?"

Cher said: "I was in Juneau, Alaska and found it. The plane that I snuck onto landed thee. I just found the boat. Because of the weather being so bad the boat was steered to Detroit, Michigan. That is how I ended up here."

Officer Jacob asked: "How did you end up in that abandoned house?"

Cher said: "I was walking westward toward Nevada when it looked like rain. The dogs came bounding out and led me into the house. When I woke up the DSPCA was standing over me. I never heard them come in. The dogs ran in and started sneezing their heads off. I felt bad that they got all wet."

Officer Jacob asked; "Do you know the breed of these dogs?"

Cher said: "They are two Chocolate Labs."

Officer Jacob asked: "Where did you learn about dogs?"

Cher said: "I spend a lot of time in libraries reading."

Officer Jacobs asked: "Where have you managed to sleep at night?"

Cher said: "Oh that's easy. I spent a night in a mall in Macy's once. That was last year. I had in the bathroom until they gates went down. I heard the rattling when that happened. Then I went to the bedding section and crawled under the covers. I slept all night like a log. I woke up just when I heard the gates going back up. I went to the bathroom and brushed my teeth. I found a store that sells toothpaste."

Officer Jacobs asked; "Why don't you give ma your tooth brush so I can give you a new one?"

Cher said: "Okay. Here it is. I think it is kind of worn out anyway. The toothpaste is almost finished May I have another tube?"

Officer Jacobs said; "Please go home with Sharon tonight. She will bring you back here tomorrow."

The next morning when Sharon woke up Cher was gone. They never heard from her again. After a medical checkup on the dogs they were adopted together by a nice family who passed the adoptions test. Mark received a phone call about Cher and was told she was a missing child. All they could do was pray for her safety.

C·H·A·P·T·E·R—12

She reappeared in Wisconsin across from Lake Huron. She ended up in Madison, Wisconsin. She walked the whole way. Madison is a city. She tried to walk west toward Nevada. Thomas McGillis was a ticket agent who was popular with the local pedestrians. Everybody knew him and respected him. He never let anybody get away with double parking or parking in front of a driveway. Peter was one of those pedestrians who looked out for Thomas's safety. One day Peter came upon a strange little girl he never saw before. He asked: "What is your name?"

The child said: "My name is Ruth."

Peter asked: "Where do you come from?"

Ruth said: "I have been alone in the world for at least three years. I don't really have anybody to take care of me."

Peter asked: "Do you go to school?"

Ruth said: "No sir. I just travel a lot and hang out in libraries. I read a lot."

Peter said: "This is my friend Jeremiah. Why don't you

let him buy you lunch and I will join you in a few minutes. I just have to make a phone call. I will be right there."

Ruth asked: "Do they have a bathroom where I can freshen up?"

Peter said: "Yes they do. It is in the back."

Ruth said: "Oh thank you sir!!"

Peter called Thomas on his cell phone outside the restaurant. He explained the situation. Thomas told him he will be right there and to hold her in his presence. He did have a requirement to call the police and children's services in the event of an incident. They all sat down together in the booth. Peter introduced Thomas to Ruth.

Thomas asked: "So Ruth. Where do you come from originally?"

Ruth said: "I honestly don't remember. I have been traveling for so long that every city is starting to look the same."

Thomas asked: "Where do you sleep at night?"

Ruth said: "I have slept in hospitals, churches, and a May's store once in a mall. I found that Catholic churches are the easiest places to hid. I waited in the confessional until the church was locked. I go to Mass on Sundays and go up to Communion. One day I ate all of the Communion Hosts before I got caught. I didn't know about the red light that was on the outside of the confessional. He threw open the curtain and startled me to death. I almost chocked on the bread."

Thomas asked: "How do you survive everyday?"

Ruth said: "I rely on the kindness of strangers. After they feed me and shelter me for the night I move on."

Thomas asked: "Have you ever flown in an airplane?"

Ruth said: "Oh yes I have flown twice."

Thomas asked: What about a cruise ship?"

Ruth said: "Yes. I have gone on a cruise ship also."

Thomas asked: "Have you ever been caught as a stowaway?"

Ruth said: "Yes. Only once when I flew to Ireland. I was caught by immigration. I was flown right back here to America."

Thomas asked: "How do you get on an airplane without a ticket and going through the metal detectors?"

Ruth said: "That is easy. I wait until the line is at its longest and sneak through the other side of the metal detectors. Those people are so overworked they can't possibly watch every inch of the hall and pay attention to what they are doing."

Thomas asked: "How did you manage to sneak onto an Aer Lingus plane?"

Ruth said: "I went to the bathroom and fell asleep. When I woke up they stewardess was banging on the door asking if I was okay."

Thomas asked: "What about libraries? You mentioned that you have slept in libraries. Have you ever been caught?"

Ruth said: "That is easy. People don't know this but in public libraries they don't even shut off all the lights. I just hide in the stacks and wait until everybody leaves. Then one time I went downstairs and found a couch to lay on. I went to sleep for the night and woke up just before everybody opened up for the day. One time I lived in the library for three days because of a hurricane or maybe it was a tornado. I watched it from the window. When I finally ventured outside there were just piles of rubble all over the place."

Rickey said: "How would you like to come home with me tonight? My wife can cook a good dinner and you can have a shower and a warm bed tonight."

Ruth said: Okay Rickey. I could use a shower. He picked up the glass and fork she was using and put it in an evidence bag. Rickey called his wife Helga and told her Peter will be bringing a child home for the evening. Ruth turned out to be a very pleasant visitor who was easy to talk to. She started to show an interest in Germany because she liked the accent Helga had.

Ruth asked: "Where are you from Helga? You speak with an accent."

Helga said; "I am from what is now called Austria."

Ruth said: "I read about a village in Austria in the valley that gets no sunlight. It is because of the mountains in the way. The residents wanted to put a mirror on the top of the mountain to get that rainbow at least."

Helga said: "You are right. New we need to go to sleep. You have had a very big day. When Rickey returned home he had an answer as to who is the real identity of Ruth. He discovered she was originally from New York. She was a missing child. Her aunt and uncle had been looking for her for at least two years. She was only six years old at the time of her mother's death. That is why she has no memory of her parents."

C-H·A·P·T·E·R—13

R uth woke up in the middle of the night and found the airport. She was on the move again. She picked a flight to Austria. It was a Lufthansa flight. She waited until the lines were long and snuck onto the plane to Austria. When she landed she found a way to circumvent the immigration line. She was puzzled by the sight of all the signs in German. She had never seen the German language before. She found herself in the Alps mountains. She spent three days wandering around the mountains and finally found a village. She thought she was back in the middle of the movie Sound of Music. She came to a monastery full of nuns and priests walking around with their hands folded. She heard an announcement that invited the tourists to join them in the chapel for Mass. She went just to look like a tourist. After Mass she spent three days returning to the airport. She took the next plane back to America. She didn't like Austria too much because nobody talked to her. She was treated like she was invisible. She managed to eat somehow.

The animals she ran into were more friendlier. One dog barked so loud and furiously that the owners had to come outside to investigate the runkus. The owner said something in German but she just ran away.

She found the airport and boarded the next plane to America. She ended up in Des Moins, Iowa.

C-H·A·P·T·E·R—14

In Des Moines she deplaned and went to the bathroom. She found the exit and brought a hot dog at a hot dog stand. She had only change in her pocket. She looked rather haggard after her long trip. The man said it was on the house. Ever since she started wandering she had been picking up pennies and loose change in the street. The man really didn't want all those pennies. She asked where were the potato farms. She was told to walk in the west direction. The man also gave her a can of soda on the house. He gave her a bottle of water to save for later. An hour later a cop drove up for lunch. The hot dog stand owner shared his story about the strange child an hour earlier. He reminded him about being near na airport. He is bound to see all kinds of characters from all over the world. The man said this was a child appeared to be traveling alone. The cop promised to be on the lookout after he took a description of the child.

She felt very refreshed after the hot dog and the soda. She walked in the direction of west. Or so she was hoping she was. Soon the skies turned dark and she needed to find shelter for the night. She found a barn that looked abandoned. The house next to the barn was dark and seemed to be empty. She entered the barn and found a lot of animals in it. There were horses, pigs, and even a donkey. She climbed a ladder and layed down in the hayloft. She went right to sleep. In the morning she was awakened by the owner of the farm. She moved and he thought it was strange that the hay was falling down around him. He climbed the ladder and found a child he had never seen before. He screamed and she screamed right back at him. He only screamed in surprise and shock. The farmer's name was John Dooley. He said: " What is your name?"

The girl said: "My name is Laura."

John asked: "How long have you been here?"

Laura said: "I came in last night. The rain drove me inside."

John asked: "I have never seen you before. Where did you come from?"

Laura said: "I am a nomad. I have been alone in the world for maybe three years or so."

John asked: "Where did you live before you were alone in the world?"

Laura said: "I don't remember. It has been so long. I think I started out in New Jersey."

John asked: "Do you go to school?"

Laura said: "No sir. I hang out in libraries during the day and read a lot."

John asked: "How do you mange to eat and shower?"

Laura said: "I rely on the kindness of strangers."

John asked: "Since you are a nomad do you have a destination specific you want to get to?"

Laura said: "I have an interest in the Mojave Desert."

John said: "You need to head west to get there. It is that way to the right of the driveway."

Laura asked: "How did you know I was up here?"

John said: "I saw the hay drop down on my head. You must have been moving around."

Laura said: "I like the idea of farm living. I thought this barn was abandoned until I came in and saw the horse. They were glad for my company."

John asked: "Have you eaten breakfast yet?"

Laura said: "No sir. I just woke up."

John said: "Help me gather the eggs and I can bring you into the house for breakfast."

The two of them gathered the eggs in one basket. Laura kept giggling because the chickens kept pecking her. She started to bleed on her hand. They left and went into the kitchen. John's sister Patty was there and John introduced her to Laura. The three of them sat down to breakfast of scrambled eggs, sausages and toast. When they finished Patty asked; "Where are you from Laura?"

Laura said: "I have been traveling the United States for so long that I don't remember anymore."

Patty asked; "How di you manage to eat?"

Laura said: "I have always relied on the kindness of strangers."

Patty asked: "How do you manage to travel?"

Laura said: "I have flown in an airplane, sailed on a cruise ship, but mostly I just walk."

Patty asked: "What are your plans for the future?"

Laura said: "Once I get to the Mojave Desert I don't know what then."

Patty asked: "What about school?"

Laura said: "If I find a school in the Mojave Desert I guess I will let them call Children's Services and put me into foster care."

Patty said: "I am surprised nobody has done that already."

Laura said: "Maybe they have, but I usually disappear into thing air after they feed me. I am small and wiry. I couldn't believe how easy it was to sneak through the metal detectors in the airports. I never brought a plane ticket, yet I have managed to fly to Ireland, and Alaska, and even Austria. I just go to the bathroom on the plane and by the time I get out we are miraculously airborne. Ireland was the only place I got caught by immigration."

Patti asked; "What about your love of animals?"

Laura said: "Animals sense that I am alone in the world. I got caught walking down the street and there was a storm coming. The animal cops found me the next day. It rained the night before and I slept right through it. The dogs came bounding into the house sneezing their heads off. The animal cops came and let us play together for about ten minutes. They brought the three of us into the animal shelter and they gave me lunch. It was hard to tell exactly whom was having more fun."

John asked: "Laura, do you remember the exact name of this place?"

Laura said: "It was in Detroit, Michigan. The place was called the Michigan Humane Society." John excused himself to go and check on the horses. Out in the barn John got the number for the Michigan Humane Society. He finally got the director on the phone after about three transfers. John explained the situation with Laura. The director remembered the child and revealed that she was a missing child from New York. He told John not to let her escape again and the detectives will be there first thing in the morning. He was told not to let her out of sight for twenty four hours. An hour later he received a phone call explaining they will be there in three days because of the snow storm in New York. All the airports are closed and getting a flight out will take a few days. All the passengers who were scheduled to fly out today were the first to be put on a plane. That was the cause of the delay. John came into the house and offered for Laura to come out and ride a horse. Laura was over the moon with delight to try it out. John instructed her on how to climb up and stay on the horse. John pulled the horse by the snout and had lead them to the Pasteur field where he was in his element. John told the horse not to make any jumps or leaps with Laura sitting on him. They just galloped around the fence. John and Patty brought 2 more horses out and the three of them went for a ride. The horses knew enough to go to the lake around the edges of the property. John helped Laura down off the horse and they had a little playtime together. After a few hours the three of them climbed back up and returned to the barn. It was almost time to start making dinner. Laura had a nice long bubble bath. John gave her a tooth brush and a new pair of sneakers. They ate hamburgers and hot dogs that night. As expected that night Laura left and vanished into think air. When John and Patti found out they sent up a prayer of hope for her safety. John called the detectives and canceled their trip. He had to explain the fact that she gave them the slip. The detectives from New York spent the next hour mapping out where she might pop up next.

C-H·a·P·T·e·R—15

Police officer Rudy McConnell was riding in his patrol car with his partner police officer Michael Davis. They had been cops with the Lincoln, Nebraska police force for about five years. They were assigned to do street patrol for the evening. Rudy fancied himself as a psychic. He said it was his third eye. They were driving down Boston Street when he suddenly screamed out "STOP!!!" This scared the daylights out of Michael and he slammed on the brakes and almost crashed the car. Michael screamed at him never to do that again.

Michael asked: "Did you get another reading?"

Rudy said: "I feel something is out of place."

Michael said: "I saw a funeral procession from St. Anne's Church last week. Maybe it is the spirit of the dead still haunting the streets."

Rudy said: "This is nothing to joke about. There is a presence here that doesn't belong here."

Michael said: "Fine. When you find this presence give

him my regards. Make him feel welcome. I am looking forward to making his acquaintance."

Rudy got out and started walking down the street. He crossed to the next street and came back again. The presence was only felt on that one street. A passer-bye stopped Rudy and started talking to him. She said she noticed a strange child in the building last night. She was almost five feet tall and very small feet carrying a backpack. She called over her daughter and showed him the approximate size and weight. When she returned from the store the child was gone.

Rudy asked: "Have you ever seen her before?"

The lady said: "No. I showed her picture to the grammar school principals in the area and nobody recognized her."

Rudy asked: "Do you still have this picture?"

The lady said: "No sir. I am sorry sir. I deleted the picture once everybody said they didn't recognize her."

Rudy said: "If you find her again try to bring her to your house for a hot meal and a warm bed. Then sneak off and call us. Sit on her if necessary."

The lady said: "Will do sir. Thank you sir."

Rudy returned to his car and Michael asked if he got any answers.. Rudy said: "Yes. I was right. There was a stranger on the block. The lady took her picture with her cell phone and sent it to the schools in the area. Everybody said they never met this child. The lady deleted the picture. She promised me she would call the cops if the child appeared again."

Michael asked: "What do you think of this story?"

Rudy said: "I honestly think we are dealing with the presence of a missing child."

Michael said: "Sadly there is nothing we can do until the child's physical body returns walking and talking. Only then can missing persons investigate.

That evening at the end of the shift meeting officer Rudy mentioned his encounter with the lady and the story of the mysterious child. The sergeant took it seriously. The sergeant told everyone to be on the lookout for her. The mysterious child was never seen or heard from again.

C-H·A·P-T-E·R—16

As expected the child found herself in the departures buildings of the International Airport. She read the departures board and picked out a Quantas Airlines plane for Australia. She found the right gate and hid in the bathroom of the plane. After they took off she came out and sat down. She eavesdropped on the stewardess and heard that they keep the last three seats open in case somebody gets sick. She just took a seat there. She hid underneath a blanket so nobody noticed her. When they landed she found herself in Sydney, Australia. When she got to the waiting room she found somebody to talk to. It was obvious she was alone and had nobody.

He said: "Excuse me madam. My name is Sinead. What is your name?"

She said: "My name is Nancy. I am here alone in the world."

Sinead said: "Why don't you come home with me?"

Nancy said: "Okay. Can I get a shower? It has been a while."

Sinead said; "Yes. You can. What are in your plans?"

Nancy said; "I don't have any plans really."

Sinead asked: "Where are you from originally?"

Nancy said: "I am from the United States. I don't really know what state I was born in. I have been alone in the world for so long now."

Sinead asked: "Do you have a passport?"

Nancy said; "I don't think so. I am not sure what that is?"

Sinead said: "It is a little blue book with your name and picture in it."

Nancy said: "No. I am going to have to say I never saw one."

Sinead asked: "What are your plans for being here?"

Nancy said: "I don't have any. I plan to just wander the streets and relocate here."

Sinead said: "Come to my house so you can get a hot mean and a good night's sleep. Right now you are considered an illegal alien. If you get caught by immigration you will be flown back to the United States."

The two of them left the airport together. When they got into the car the first thing Nancy noticed was that the cares are driven on the other side of the road.

Sinead said: "Oh yes. America is the only place in the world that drives on the right hand side of the road. We drive on the left, but our steering wheel is on the right."

Nancy said: "It looks awkward to me."

Sinead said: "Oh you get used to it. I have lived here all my life, so this looks natural to me. What do you want to do tomorrow to start seeing our beautiful land?"

Nancy said: "I saw on TV that you have a bridge people can climb."

Sinead said: "Oh yes. I can take you there tomorrow and climb with you. There is a pedestrian staircase you can use. There is also a guide giving lectures about its history. After that I can take you to the zoo."

When they arrived at his house it was to a 3rd floor walk up. He unlocked the door and was greeted by his Cocker Spaniel, Collie mixed breed dog. He was a very friendly dog. As soon as she sat down on the ourch she fell asleep. Sinead called his boss Olaf from the bedroom. He arranged to meet Olaf at the zoo at 11:00 the next morning. What Nancy didn't know was the Sinead was an undercover immigration officer. His job was o hang out and stop people from sneaking into the country illegally. They formulated a plan to meet up without raising suspicians. The next morning Sinead got up early to feed Nancy her breakfast. They were at the bridge by 8:00. They were the first in line. It was a small group because most of Australia don't wake up before noon. Nancy had no shortness of breath when she got to the top. She was teasing Sinead because he was out of breath. They took five minutes to take in the view. She was flabbergasted by it all. Going down was just as dizzying as going up. At 11:00 Sinead and Nancy sat down on a bench and ate a funnel cake with a log of sugar. Sinead said: "We are waiting for my friend Olaf to meet us. He will walk around with us and see the animals.

Since we live here we can show you interesting things. Here he comes now."

Olaf said: "Hi Sinead. How are you today?"

Sinead said: "I am fine today. I want you to meet a friend of mine Nancy. She is from America."

Nancy said; "We had some funnel cake left. Do you want a piece?"

Olaf said: "Ooh yeah!!! Thank you. I love funnel cake. I don't usually eat it because it is such big portions. All that sugar going into you is enough to make you climb the side of a building."

Nancy said: "Sinead said you and him work together. What exactly do you do?"

Olaf said: "We are chefs who opened a cooking school together. We are off now for the summer. We are open only from September to June. Our specialty is people coming here for vacation and hang out in our kitchen. When they are not in clas sthey are free to do anything they want."

Nancy said: "That sounds different. When can I sign up?"

Olaf said: "You have to be twenty one to sign up. You also have to prove you are legal."

Nancy asked: "What do you mean by that?"

Olaf said: "You have to show us a passport."

Nancy asked: "What is that thing staring at me from the tree? All I see is orange eyes and a tail."

Olaf laughed and said: "That is a Koala Bear. He is perfectly harmless. He is just a little shy of people."

Nancy said: "He kind of looks like a raccoon. That is something we have in America. Raccoons have a complete opposite reputation than these Koala Bears. When you see a raccoon you run inside the house and hide. They will eat your garbage and leave a mess in your yard. There is nothing you can do to get rid of them."

Sinead said: "It has been a long day. Whey don't we go back to my house and Olaf and I will cook you one of our specialties."

Nancy said: "Sounds good. What are you cooking?"

Sinead said: "A whole turkey, mashed potatoes, and carrots. We eat very healthy around here."

Olaf said; "Give me your hand so we don't get separated. Our next stop is the supermarket. They merrily went off and brought the food that was necessary for their evenings plans. Sinead pushed the cart around while Olaf looked for a Butterball Turkey. He read the tags until he found one that said 10 lbs. For three people that was plenty. Olaf next walked them over to get the turkey bags. Just another ingredient needed. They finished getting everything and got into line. When nobody was looking Sinead snuck in a bag of dog food and dog treats. He always got under Olaf's skin when he did that. They arrived back in Sinead's house and Sinead said that Nancy should go in the room and take a nap. It had been a long. Day. Nancy decided to take a long hot bath first. When Nancy went in the room for a nap Olaf and Sinead started talking about this child from seemingly nowhere. Olaf was impressed with the story Sinead dreamed up to catch this illegal alien. They both knew in their heart that she has someone looking for her. They just couldn't prove it just yet. The last thing they wanted was for her to get spooked and vanish again. Three and a half hours later they were sitting around the table with the turkey and the whole meal. Olaf mashed the potatoes with the electronic whipper. They all feasted like never before. The two men cleaned up and Nancy went to bed. She left in the middle of the night because she was afraid of all this talk about illegal aliens. She ended up on a plane back to the United States.

C-H·A·P·T·E·R—17

She landed in a city called Cheyenne, Wyoming. Nobody seemed to notice her at the airport, so she just wandered through to the street. She looked around and saw a trolley. She climbed to the top of the mountain. She looked down and saw a lot of horses running wild. They trolley was a lot easier than walking the far. They trolley stopped to let the passengers watch the show. It was free. When they got off everybody was herded into the arena for a rodeo show. They had bull riding and horse corralling. An announcement came over the loudspeaker and announced what was happening. The horses were not being harmed by the rope around the neck. Tourists were very common in the arena at that time of year. Nothing about her stood out. Other patrons thought it was strange a child would be there alone. The father of one family notified security. Security came in and talked to the child. He said: "Excuse me little lady. What is your name?"

The child said: "My name is Megan. What is your name?"

He said: "My name is Sean. Are you a tourist?"

Megan said: "Yes sir. I am a tourist."

Sean asked: "Where are you from?"

Megan said: "I am alone in the world. I have been wandering the United States."

Sean asked: "What happened to your parents?"

Meagan said; "I don't remember them."

Sean asked: "What state are you from originally?"

Megan said: "I don't remember."

Sean asked; "How did you get here?"

Megan said: "This time I flew in an airplane from Australia It was from Quantas airlines. I have flown several times."

Sean asked: "How do you manage to fly unsupervised and without a ticket?"

Meagan said: "I sneak onto the plane and hide in the bathroom. I also sneak through the metal detectors. I wait until the officers are at their busiest then just walk through."

Sean asked: "How do you manage to eat?"

Megan said: "I rely ont eh kindness of strangers. People feel sorry for me when I tell them I am alone in the world. They are quick to open their homes to me. I stay just long enough for a shower and a warm bed. I usually disappear in the night."

Sean asked: "When you are walking the streets how do you manage to go to the bathroom?"

Megan said: "I am usually good at minding a mall

nearby. Sometimes I have to use a restaurant. I just sneak in unnoticed."

Sean asked: "Since you sneak through metal detectors how you ever been caught?"

Megan said: "Only in Ireland. I got caught by immigration. They put me on a plane back to America. They left me in a room with bunk beds. They had an officer sitting in a chair with the chair sitting up against the door. When his shift was over another woman came in and did the same thing. She could see the wheels turning in my head, but I just couldn't come up with anything. They fed me three square meals which was the best food I ever ate. The officer held my hand until I sat in the seat next to a man. She buckled me in and left the plane."

Sean asked: "What about going to school?"

Megan said; "I hang out in libraries and read a lot. I manage to go in just before closing and hide in the stacks. Then I have someplace quiet and warm to sleep. There is usually a bench to stretch out in. I escape in the morning. Luckily I haven't been caught."

Sean asked: "Why don't you stop and enroll yourself in school? You seem like you can come up with any kind of believable story."

Megan said: "I don't have a permanent address. I also need my parents signature on the forms. I is illegal to forge signatures of dead people."

Sean said: "You are right about forging signatures. How old are you anyway?"

Megan said: "I think I am around 11 years old. I don't even know when is my birthday."

The man sitting behind them had a tape recorder in his hand recording the conversation. Sean said: "Megan, why don't you go home with him? I have known this guy since high school. I can assure you he won't bother you tonight. He is here with his wife and children."

Megan said: "Okay. I guess I can do that. When they arrived home Megan was given a shower and a hot meal. She spent some time playing Monopoly with the family. It didn't take her long to catch on to how to play. After an hour the father excused himself to make a phone call. He called his sergeant on the phone and explained the mysterious appearance of this child. He did a computer search and discovered that she was in fact a missing child from Orange County in upstate New York. Her family reported her missing after the funeral of her mother. They lived in Manhattan at the time of this occurrence. The sergeant mailed the audio tape to the New York Detectives overnight delivery. When they played it for Megan's aunt and uncle there was no question about who was on the tape. It was definitely their niece.

CHAPTER—18

As usual in the middle of the night Megan left for parts unknown. This time she found herself in a freight train yard. This was a first time for her. She climbed on top of a car and entered through the open door. She hid behind boxes in a dark corner. Somebody came by and closed the door. She looked over and found two pairs of eyes staring back at her. She stared back at them startled.

She asked: "Who are you?"

The gentlemen answered: "My name is Marion, this is my friend Tyrone. Now you can tell us who you are."

The girl said: "My name is Sally. What are you doing here?"

Marvin said: "We are known as rail riders. We are homeless from a building collapse. We lost our jobs because of absenteeism. All we did was try to put our lives back together. We joined the rail riders for lack of anything else to do. We were neighbors.

Sally asked; "What about your families?"

Marvin said; "We were never married. We both lived alone. We can't get unemployment because we have no permanent address."

Sally asked: "Where are we headed to?"

Marvin said: "We never know. When the train stops we jump off. We stay in whatever town the train stops in. Sometimes the train workers run through and make sure there are no stowaways. We hide and watch out and then jump on after the train starts. It is a little dangerous, but the risk is well worth it."

Sally asked: "Have you ever been caught?"

Tyrone said: "Once I was caught. But I ran like my pants were on fire. He was patrolling one side of the doors , but I jumped on the other side of the car. I got scraped up, but my body healed. I met up with Marvin at the next stop. He was in the next car. Then we stayed together ever since."

Sally asked: "How do you eat?"

Tyrone said: "That is the tricky part of this kind of life. Whenever we jump off there doesn't seem to be a restaurant or men's room anywhere."

Marvin said: "Now you tell us about your life Sally. How did you manage to find yourself in a situation like this?"

Sally said: "I am alone in the world. I left the house of the latest person and found myself on this train. Where are we headed for?

Marvin said: "We never know. Whenever the train stops we jump off if the spirit moves us."

Sally asked: "How do you manage to eat?"

Marvin said: "Sometimes we open the boxes in front of us. It tends to be fruit being transported to the different supermarkets around the country. How do you eat?"

Sally said: "I rely on the kindness of strangers. People are always giving me food. I pick up pennies from the street."

Marvin and Tyrone both laughed and said: "Gee we never thought of that. How many do you usually find?"

Sally said: "About five a day on a good day. I steal a lot of fruit from fruit stands which is something I am not proud of. But sometimes you gotta do what you gotta do to survive. Sometimes I pull out all that change from my pocket and I get to eat for free."

At that point the train stopped and they all jumped out. They found themselves in Houston, Texas. She parted ways with Marvin and Tyrone. She found herself wandering into a barn. She didn't know that she was at the Houston ASPCA and that she was sleeping with the horses that were up for adoption. There wasn't anyone around, so she walked into one of the stalls and layed down to sleep. The horse didn't seem to mind the company. At first Sally talked nice and put the horse at ease with her presence. It was very clean. The staff just cleaned it about a half hour before Sally's arrival. The other hourse across the way was upset about the presence of an intruder. His instinct was to attract attention that something was amiss in the barn. There was a part of the building across the way that was monitored 24/7/ It was the hospital and surgical suite. There was a surgery going on. The entrance to that was through the arrivals dock. The horse bolted and trotted across the way. There was a poker game going on in the hospital suite. Their job was to keep checking the sick animals and make sure they don't turn critical or actually die on them. They heard the skip-klop of horse shoes coming down the hall, but they thought they were imagining it. The weather was turning windy outside, so they just assumed that was what they were hearing. The door opened unexpectedly. Four people screamed bloody murder and all the cards went flying all over the place when they looked up and saw the horse standing in the doorway neighing at them. The two men in the surgical suite ran out to see what was wrong. They almost slipped on the floor skidding to a stop. The horse appeared to be in distress. The surgeon took the horse by the muzzle and tried to calm him down. The assistant look din the room and told the four people to breathe. They were all in a state of shock. The horse was led back to bed so to speak. The other horses were watching the show from the sides of their eyes. He looked in all the stables and checked them out for anything amiss. The last stable he checked was the one Sally was hiding out in. She was crouched in the corner. The doctor entered and the horse went ballistic. No way was Sally going anywhere with her on guard. The surgeon left the barn for his own safety. In the morning the surgeon told a staff member to go and check the stables for intruders. Sure enough there was Sally sleeping like a baby in the same stall as last night. The staff member walked into the stall and said: "Hi there. What is your name?"

The girl said: "My name is Nancy."

The staff member said: "My name is Christine. How id you get here?"

Nancy said: "I rode a freight train with a rail rat. Actually there were two of them."

Christine asked: "Where did you board this freight train?"

Nancy said: "I don't remember."

Christine asked: "How did you find this place?"

Nancy said: "I jumped off the train when it stopped and found this barn. I was wondering when the horse show will begin."

Christine said: "These animals are all up for adoption."

Nancy said; "In the last place I was at there was a horse show in an arena. They were doing tricks and all. There was a rope thrown around the horse's neck."

Christine said: "That is called a lasso. It doesn't hurt the horses. By the way. Where are your parents?"

Nancy said: "Both of my parents are dead. I have been alone in the world, so I just wander around. I rely on the kindness of strangers. They feed me and give me shelter."

Christine asked: "Have you ever stayed in a shelter for the homeless?"

Nancy said: "No. In desperation I sleep inside hospitals and libraries."

Christine said: "Why don't you come with me and get some breakfast?"

Nancy said: "Okay. I probably should use the bathroom too."

Christine ordered breakfast and introduced Nancy to the whole office. Nancy ate her usual eggs and sausage. After talking to Nancy the adoption head named Michael guessed that she came from Cheyenne Wyoming. He made a phone call to the train station about where the latest freight train came from. This was confirmed for sure. The dispatcher also confirmed that rail rats are a big problem and one that is difficult to conquer. The surgeon from last night walked in and found Nancy. Christine introduced her as the intruder from last night. The surgeon asked: "How did you get in?"

Nancy said: "I walked in. the door was open. And by the way what is your name anyway/?"

The surgeon said: "My name is Paul."

Christine asked: "Since you said you were alone in the world what is your destination?"

Nancy said; "I am trying to make it to Nevada. I want to see the Mojave Desert."

Christine asked: "What do you plan to eat in the desert?"

Nancy said: "I haven't thought about that. I guess I will cross that bridge when I come to it." That night Nancy went home with Paul for a hot bath and a good dinner. She left in the middle of the night to continue her journey. Fortunately the weather was all clear. She jumped on to a freight car and hid until it started to move. When she jumped off she found herself in Tulsa, Oklahoma. Before she left the last thing Paul said to her was that she needed suntan lotion for sunburn.

CHAPTER—19

When she jumped off it was morning the next day. Nobody noticed her lurking around. She brought a hot pretzel with way too much salt on it. She ate it anyway. She found this to be a very nice city. She walked to main street and found herself in the Grand Ole Opry House. She sat in the last row because there was a rehearsal for a country music concert. The lead singer of a band walked in and noticed her just inside the door. He said: "Hi there little lady. What is your name?"

The girl answered: "My name is Wanda. What is your name?"

He said: "My name is Trey. It is a came from the south. I don't like my name at all. I go by the nickname Trevor. What brings you to the Grand Ole Opry House?"

Wanda said; "I am a nomad. I just wander around from place to place."

Trey asked: "Where are your parents?"

Wanda said: "I have none. I am alonc in the world."

Secretly she was getting tired of telling this story, but she went on with it.

Trey asked; "Where do you live during the school year?"

Wanda said: "I just said I am a nomad. That means I don't stay in one place for very long."

Trey asked: "Do you have a specific destination in mind?"

Wanda said: "I am trying to make it to the Mojave Desert. I want to live there."

Trey asked; "What about school?"

Wanda said: "I haven't thought of that yet. All I really need is a library to read books all day."

Trey asked; "What makes you think there are any kind of buildings in the desert? Have you ever considered that it might be all vacant land?"

Wanda said: "No. I haven't thought of that either." Wanda walked out of the theatre and never looked back. She was not impressed with Tulsa, Oklahoma. She didn't realize that Trey was just trying to help. He always came across as a nasty bully. It was just his personality, but underneath it all he was as soft as a twinkie. He was divorced two times because of it. Nobody knew how to take him. He didn't have too many friends in town. Three female assistants also quit on him. He just had to pray for her safety and hope she made it to the Mojave Desert.

CHAPTER—20

She went out in the middle of the night and found herself back at the rail yards with the freight trains being loaded up. She jumped into another car and hid in the darkened corner. The train finally started to move. She had no idea where she was headed. The train stopped a few times to unload its cargo, but she slept deeply right through it. When she woke up the first time she noticed somebody had closed the door. She couldn't see out the one window. It was too high for her. She didn't care where she was going. Any place would be better than Tulsa, Oklahoma. She didn't understand that not all residents are like that. She just happened to have run into somebody that rubbed her the wrong way. In reality he didn't mean her any harm. When she finally jumped off she saw a sign that said Welcome to Portland, Oregon. She brought a can of diet Pepsi and a bag of pretzels from a snack stand. She watched where everybody was going. She followed the crowd. They were all headed up a mountain into a ranger park. She wandered in there and found a duck pond. She saw a duck and a Black Lab checking each other out. It was adorable to see the dog barking at the duck and the duck quacking back at the dog. They looked like they were playing with each other. She couldn't help but cackle and giggle at the show. Wanda didn't hear the park ranger coming up behind her. The guy in the snack cottage called him to alert him that there was an unsupervised child in the park. He knew the one right away because the clerk described her exactly. He walked up behind her and when she turned around she almost jumped out of her skin.

He said: "Hi there my lady. My name is David. What is your name?"

She said; "My name is Peggy. I didn't hear you come up behind me."

David said: "You seem to be engrossed staring at the duck and the dog. Aren't they adorable together?"

Peggy said: "Yes. I didn't know different animals can be friends with each other. I thought dogs were only friends with other dogs."

David said: "That happens all other the animal kingdom. Where are you parents?"

Peggy said: "Both of my parents are dead. I have nobody in this world to speak for me."

David asked: "Where do you live?"

Peggy answered: "I have no home. I have been traveling the United States for almost tow years now. I have flown overseas three times. I only got caught once in Ireland for not having a passport. Truthfully I didn't even know what that was."

David asked: "How did you fly in an airplane without a ticket or ID?"

Peggy said: "That was the easy part. I waited until the staff was at their busiest and then slipped by the metal detectors unnoticed. Nobody was watching the unmanned station at the very end."

David asked; "How did you get on the airplane without showing your ticket?"

Peggy said: "That was also easy as pie. I waited until they loaded the plane with food and the kitchen was on the left. I went right to the bathroom and fell asleep."

David said: "You are pretty smart and clever for such a young child. Exactly how old are you anyway?"

Peggy said: "I honestly am not sure. It has been so long since I have seen my family nobody has ever told me. I assume I am somewhere between ten and twelve years old."

David asked: "Do you have hair on your body?"

Peggy said: "No. Not at all. Only on my head."

David asked: "You say you travel the United States. How do you survive?"

Peggy said: "I have met some very nice people. As soon as people hear I am alone in the world they are quick to open their homes to me. I stay just long enough for a nice shower and a good hot meal. Then I leave in the middle of the night just as mysteriously as I appeared. People must scratch their heads the next day wondering if that was real. Was there really a little girl in their house?"

David asked: "How else have you traveled within these United States?"

Peggy said: "I have traveled by freight cars but more walking than anything else. I tried to walk west toward the Mojave Desert. That is where I want to settle in. Somebody told me it might be vacant land and no schools. Is that true?"

David said: "No. There is Las Vegas, North Las Vegas, and Laughlin. There you have it. Thee cities to choose from."

Peggy said: "I knew that guy was full of beans. Somebody told me it is all vacant land. By the way. Have you ever heard of a rail rat?"

David said: "Yes. Those are people who ride the rails everyday. They have no homes or jobs, so no connections with anybody. Have you ever met one?"

Peggy said: "I have met two of them. How do they become one?"

David said: "Usually it is just that they lost their job. They can't pay their rent so they get evicted. You can't get unemployment because you don't have a permanent address. A lot of people don't plan on that kind of life, but fate deals them that card. They aren't all drug dealers. You should just pray for them. They usually don't mean any harm."

Peggy said: "That is what they said. It must be true then."

David asked: "Have you ever been assaulted?"

Peggy said: "No sir. I have never been assaulted. People don't touch me, but give me attitude."

David asked: "How do you plan on getting to the Mojave Desert?"

Peggy said: "Can you point me in the direction of southeast?"

David turned her around and said: "That way. Just keep walking. You will get there soon enough."

Peggy said: "Thanks. It was nice meeting you."

She kept walking and found herself near the airport. She read the board and picked a destination that said Iceland. It was an Icelander plane. She figured it would be cold, but she didn't care. She went through her usual airport routine and landed in Iceland about five hours later.

C-H-A-P-T-E-R—21

When she got off the plane she started wandering the streets. She came upon somebody that said he was the dean of students from the university. He spoke Engliksh very well and appeared to be an American. He said: "Hi there. My name is Lenny. What is your name?"

She said: "My name is Stacy.

Lenny said: "What brings you over here to Iceland?"

Stacy said: "I am alone in the world. Back in America I have nobody to speak for me."

Lenny said: "Why don't you come with me? I can take you to the cafecteria and you can have a hot meal. Have you slept yet?"

Stacy said: "Yes sir. I have slept on the plane. I didn't wake up until we started to land. That is why I didn't wake up until we started to land. That is why I am wide awake."

Lenny said: "I will take you to eat a typical American meal. Just stick with me kid."

Stacy smiled and said: "Oh thank you Lenny."

She was shocked to see a McDonalds all the way up here in Iceland. Lenny said: "We will not go to McDonalds right now. We can save that for lunch tomorrow."

They arrived at the cafecteria and he ordered a 3 piece chicken and French fries for her. He got a hamburger for himself and a French fries. The hamburger was thick as thieves. They sat at a table and wolfed down her food very fast. He went back to get a diet pepsi for her and a coffee for himself. Ever since he came to Iceland he has been drinking more and more hot liquids.

Stacy asked: "If you are an American how did you end up in Iceland?"

Lenny said: "I lost my job in Boston because of budget cuts. Rather than go on unemployment I took the next plane to Iceland and took over. They needed someone right away because the pervious guy got drunk and froze to death outside his house. His wife found him the next morning."

Stacy said: "When I went to Australia he asked me if I have a work visa. Don't you need one here?"

Lenny said: "Every country has its own rules about that. In Iceland if you breath and can tolerate the weather you can work here. You just have to prove you are at least twenty one years old. Tomorrow I will take you to do a little sight seeing. For tonight just go to sleep."

In the morning they got up and ate a home cooked breakfast of scrambled eggs and toast. They drove over to a certain spot that was popular with the tourists. There was hot water coming out of the ground. It bubbled up like a volcano.

They couldn't get too close because they would have been scalded. Stacy couldn't figure that one out for the life of her. Ice cold land on top and boiling water underneath it. They left that spot and drove to McDonalds for lunch. She sat in on a college class.

Lenny arranged for her to speak to a counselor while he was in a meeting. She was given a typical IQ test. She scored an astounding 180. He had to check the numbers and answers four times to make sure he got it right. Stacy got nervous about all the questions and left in the middle of the night. They airport was pretty close by. She learned from the previous years that she should follow in the direction that the airplanes are flying. Then the airport will come into view. She knew the airport by the tower. She snuck up there once to check it out. She saw just a bunch of people watching dots moving around on computer screens. She left pretty quickly. She watched the departures board and managed to board a plane to Montreal, Canada.

C·H·A·P·T·E·R—22

In Montreal she left the plane and started wandering around. She found it to be a beautiful city. All the houses were very colorful and pretty. It looked like a colonial town. She wandered into a mall that was an inside mall. She waled through and her eyes almost fell out of her head. She actually saw a beach inside. It had sand and waves and all. Her heart almost stopped when she saw somebody jump from a platform. She didn't see the bungi cord the person was attached to. She had a bathing suit, but she was too shy to put it on. She walked up to the food court. She ate her usual chicken fingers.

Meanwhile elsewhere in the mall upstairs in the Eddie Bauer store there was a huge ruckus going on. Security was called there to arrest a shoplifter. He was not a very nice person at all. The cops get there and scream at the suspect to dro the merchandise. He refuses and security pulls their guns out an points at him. He clearly had nowhere to go. He shocked everybody when he jumped over the railing and landed on a chair right at Stacy's table. He picked her up and pointed a gun at her head. He told the cops to back off or he will put a bullet in the kid's head.

Stacy knew the right move next. She yelled: "Oh goody. Are you taking care of me for a while? Can you buy me new shoes and new clothes?"

The shoplifter yelled: "Shut up!!! No Talking!!!"

His name was Elvin. All the cops stood around scratching their heads not sure what to make of it.

Stacy said: "Before we leave you have to let me go to the bathroom."

Elvin yelled: "I said shut up!! What part of the don't you understand?"

She knocked the gun out of his hand. When he picked it up she gave him a swift kick in the seat of his pants. Then she gave him what is known as a SING. Eye sockets, Instep, Nose, Groin. By the time he recovered she was gone like the wind and he was in handcuffs. One cop grabbed her and pulled her to safety. The forensics team stood at the railing and tried to lift fingerprints. They also tried to lift prints from the gun that he dropped. He was arrested and held without bail. Two weeks later he was indicted on weapons charges and kidnapping and endangering the welfare of a child. He was 20 years old and got off scott free. His hostage disappeared into thin air. The testimony of ten cops as eyewitnesses wasn't enough to convict him. About a month later the sergeant asked about the hostage. The results of the finger print test showed shocking results. One print showed the presence of a missing child. She found herself at a Shortline Bus Station. She boarded one bus that was packed and layed down in the back seat and went to sleep. When she woke up and found herself in Salt Lake City, Utah.

Chapter 23

Ryan O'Connor was having the worst day of his life. He was a thirteen year old ninth grader who was called to the principal's office. The minute he saat down he started crying hysterically and bawling his eyes out like a baby. The principal's name was Steven O'Donnell. Steven couldn't get a word in edge wise. After ten minutes he asked: "What happened in woodshop yesterday?"

Between his tears he said: "I left class early. I am afraid of failure and I don't understand how to use the instruments."

Steven asked; "Why don't you ask the teacher for help?"

Ryan said: "I don't want to look like I am not keeping up."

Steven said: "We can forget about this if you do one thing. You cannot go unpunished for this transgression. Go lay down in the nurses' office. I will have to call your mother and send you home for the day. She will come and pick you up. As far as she will know you have a stomach flu brought on by stress. She doesn't have to know anything about you leaving class early."

Ryan said: "Thank you sir. I promise this will never happen again."

Steven said: "Go!!!" Get thyself to the nurse. He jumped up and ran. The secretary followed him and told the nurse what was wrong with him. She returned to the office and got out Ryan's phone number. Ryan's mother told him she will be right over to pick him up. She arrived about twenty minutes later and was led straight to the principal's office. Mr. O'Donnell went to get Ryan from the nurse's office. The three of them seated themselves in Steven's office and Steven started to explain that Ryan ahs a nervous stomach and he got sick in school this morning. He suggested she put him to bed at 7:00 that night right after giving him chicken soup. He is expected to do all his homework. Mrs. O'Conner thanked him for taking care of him. The next day Steven was sitting in his office when he had a special surprise visitor to his office. It was a young lady who wanted to register for classes. Steven asked: "What is your name?"

The child answered: My name is Marcia Duncan." She pulled that name out of a hat from the Dunkin Donuts coffee sitting on his desk.

Steven asked: "Where is your address?"

Marcia said: "My address is 1500 Vine Street." That was the address of the Payless Shoe Store on the next corner in the strip mall.

Steven asked: "Where are your parents?"

Marcia said: "I am alone in the world. I want to make

sure I get an education. I know I can't get anywhere without one."

Steven said: "That is true. How did you lose your parents?"

Marcia said: "I have been homeless for tow years now. I just woke up one morning and they were gone. I have been wandering the United States ever since."

Steven told her to follow him to class. He showed up at Ryan's classroom and started talking to the class. He asked Ryan to step outside for a chat.

Steven asked: "Please give me your mother's phone number where I can reach her. I promise you this has nothing to do with you. This is just two adults talking about something that has nothing to do with children."

Ryan said: "The number is in my cell phone in my locker." He got it and put the call through.

Steven said; "That girl that came in here with me is a new student in this school. I decided to make my life easier and have her have the same schedule as you. She will follow you around. Now get back to class."

Ryan said: "Yes sir. Thank you sir."

Steven got Mrs. O'Connor to come over to the school. He promised Ryan was fine and not in any trouble. When she arrived she was asked to sit down with Steven.

He opened by saying: "Good morning Mrs. O'Connor. Thank you for coming in. As I said on the phone this meeting has nothing to do with Ryan. I have a special favor to ask of you. I have a new student who appeared in my office seemingly out of the blue. She tells me she is an orphan, but my gut feeling is that there is more to her story than that."

Mrs. O'Connor said: "Of course Mr. O'Donnell. I would be glad to help you out with this."

Steven said: "Oh thank you madam. Please take her home with you tonight and give her a hot shower and a nutritious meal. I think she might be a missing child. I just can't prove it yet."

Mrs. O'Connor suggested giving her a cup to drink out of. She needed to hand it over to the police for DNA testing. If her DNA is in the missing persons database then we have a hit. I just don't want to make her suspicious of anything. Have the plain clothes police here in the morning. I will bring you a cup that she drank out of."

Steven said: "You're a genius."

That night Marcia and Ryan were at the dinner table. Marcia met Ryan's father. He ate dinner in a juit jacket and tie. Marcia had never seen that before. His name was Jeremy.

Jeremy said: "So Ryan. I know I have been out of town lately. How are you liking your new school?"

Ryan said: "I like it. Yesterday I was sent home early because I threw up my breakfast. The principal looked at me and I lost my breakfast. He thinks I just have a nervous stomach."

Jeremy said: "You take after me Ryan. I always had that problem. Your mother also has that problem. That is how we first met in the eighth grade/ You are a true Irishman. Just try to drink water at every opportunity. It will help your insides function properly. Who is your friend here?"

Marcia said: "My name is Marcia. I am an orphan. I just walked into the principal's office and tried to register. The principal called Ryan's mother and I came here for the night."

Jeremy asked: "What happened to your parents?"

Marcia said: "I have no memory of anybody. I just woke up one day and they were gone."

Mrs. O'Connor chimed in and said: "Marcia, I set up the bathroom with clean towels and a clean washrag. Pleae get in the shower and get comfortable for the evening. Don't forget to wash your hair."

Marcia said: "Oh thank you Mrs. O'Connor."

Mrs. O'Connor said: "Don't forget we have three other people around here. Please don't take too long in there. Ryan will show you where the bathroom is. I also brought you a spare package of underwear. I guessed at the size. Just use one of those."

Marcia said: "Okay Mrs. O'Connor."

That night after Marcia and Ryan were in bed Mrs. O'Connor took her husband out on the lawn to talk about their week. Mr. O'Connor asked: "What do you make of the mysterious appearance of Marcia?"

Mrs. O'Connor said: "I think she is a missing child, but we can't prove that yet. That is why I will bring a mug to school tomorrow that she drank out of."

The next morning the kids got ready for school. There was no dilly-dallying in the O'Connor household in the mornings. Ryan knew that from the first grade. That simply was not tolerated. He never challenged his mother on that issue.

Mrs. Ryan had the cup that Marcia drank out of. She went to the principal's office and handed it in to Steven. The plain clothes cop took the cup and told them they would have an answer in three days. Marcia went in the front door but slipped out the back unnoticed. She once again vanished into thin air. The algebra teacher asked of her whereabouts. Ryan said she might be in the bathroom. He knows she couldn't have gotten lost. She was never seen again. A few days later they had a definite ID on the girl. A missing child from New York. Ryan and his family could only pray for the child's safety. Ryan graduated 3 years later with honors. He really tried to keep his grades up. He was glad to be rid of workshop. He never got over his fear of the instruments. The day after he graduated he finally admitted to what really happened on that fateful day in Freshman year when he had his first stomach flu. His mother told him not to worry about it. It wasn't a big deal. He kept his promise to the principal to stay out of trouble and never do that again.

Chapter 24

She finally crossed the border into Nevada. She started looking for the desert. The first place she found was a town called Leihigh, Nevada. That had a lot of casinos, but plenty of food to eat. She didn't eat the crabs because she didn't like looking at the claws. The Sushi didn't look attractive either. She went for the chicken as usual. It was fried chicken, but not overly greasy. She had plenty of mashed potatoes too. Somebody came over and poured her a glass of water. She slipped out the back and sat down on the stone slab and watched the Colorado River flow by. There was a tour boat going by. People stopped and waved to her. She smiled and waved back. The sun was very hot so she assumed she had made it to the desert. She saw cacti in the road. She cut herself on the needles. The top of it felt very furry like it was growing hair. She walked into a cave to spend the night. It was getting late in the afternoon and the chill was creeping into the air. She saw bats flying around over her head. She came out and saw mores tars than she could count. She was fascinated by that. She found water dripping down the walls of the cave. She figured out to open her mouth and let the water drip in. It took too long because it was just a drop at a time. Outside the cae somebody dropped a cigarette lighter. She figured out how to use it and brought it inside with her. She was astonished that there was writing on the wall. She followed the arrow and found a light. She found an elderly couple sitting in lounge chairs watching television. What she stumbled on was a cave converted into somebody's living quarters. She never knew that was possible The man was a retired engineer and electrician, and his son worked with him for about three months. Working around the clock the job was finished in no time flat. The husband name was Donald. His wife's name was Arlene. He was fascinated by the presence of this unexpected visitor. Donald said: "Well hello there little lady. What is your name?"

The girl said; "My name is Janet."

Donald asked: "How did you find this place?"

Janet said: "I was wandering around outside and got chilly. I came in to the cave and found the lights on. Then I found you. Where exactly am I?"

Arlene said: "This is the Mojave desert. My husband lost his job, so we lost our home. Instead of being homeless my husband and son put this together. They presented it to me for our 50th wedding anniversary. He wanted to remain busy and not become bored or idle. Where exactly are you from?"

Janet said: "I don't really come from anywhere. I am

alone in the world. I have been traveling the United Sates for about two years now. My parents I believe are dead."

Donald asked: "How do you survive?"

Janet said: "As soon as I tell people that I am alone in the world they are only too happy to open their homes to shelter and feed me. Then I vanish in the middle of the night."

Donald asked: "Why do you vanish in the middle of the night?"

Janet said: "I don't like to stay too long in one place. I had dreams of living in the Mojave Desert. I didn't know there were actual city's in the desert where a lot of people live. Where did you live when your husband was working on this?"

Arlene said: "We lived in Leighigh in one of the casino hotels. My husband and son went out everyday, so I just stayed behind. Living in the desert you have to drink a lot of water to prevent dehydration. You look as though you could use some tea."

Janet asked: "May I have something to eat?"

Arlene said: "Of course Janet. I will make you some scrambled eggs and toast." She excused herself to the kitchen and started making that meal. When she was gone Donald asked: "What about school Janet?"

Janet said: "I registered for the ninth grade, but took off after one night. I also spent a lot of time in libraries reading. I spent time in hospitals and in the stacks of libraries. Usually there is a couch in libraries. I wait until closing time and stretch out and go to sleep. I don't think I have ever slept on the streets. I have traveled overseas a few times."

Donald asked; "Do you have a passport?"

Janet said: "No. But immigration only caught me once in Ireland. Usually I slip past everyone because I am small and wiry. Nobody can watch every spot in the airport."

Arlene returned to with her meal. She went right to sleep. When Donald went to sleep she slipped out unnoticed. When she exited the cave it was daylight again. Ronald and Arlene had no knowledge of contacting police, so when Janet vanished they just prayed for her safety. Arlene started to wonder if Janet was real or if they were both dreaming. They concluded that she was real because they both had the same dream and remembered the same details. Donald told his son about this. He didn't know what to make of it either.

C-H-a-p-t-e-r—25

Janet came out and started walking. She followed the road between the mountains and ended up in the small town of Eli, Nevada. She wandered into the outskirts at first and found a drug store with many new things in it. She found something called Dippitty Doo, a hair product. The jar said it was a hair relaxer. She had no idea what that meant. She sat at the counter and ordered something called a chocolate egg cream. She emptied her pockets of the change. He thought she was a tourist that got lost. She said the chocolate egg cream was heavenly. In walked the sherriff with his dog a Siberian Husky. It appeared as though the dog led the sherriff into the store and straight to Janet. He sat down on the stool next to Janet and the sherriff had to knock him down. The sherriff sat down on the stool next to janet. He said: "Hi there little lady. What is your name?"

Janet said: "My name is Martha."

The sherriff said: "My name is Joseph. It is nice to meet you Martha. Are you a tourist that got lost?"

Martha said: "No sir. I am a wanderer who is traveling the United States. I am alone in the world."

Joseph said: "My dog seems to be attracted to you. Would you like to come home with me for shelter?"

Martha said: "Oh yes sir. You are a policeman, so I guess you are a safe person to go with."

The dog let out a bark of excitement and gave his paw to shake hands. Joseph laughed and said the dog wanted a new playmate. They took off in the police car. The dog and Martha in the back seat. He started panting with excitement. They arrived at the sherriff's office for a few minutes. Everybody was surprised to find the sherriff coming in on a Saturday. Martha was given a toy to throw at the dog and the two of them walked into a windowless room to play catch in. The dog kept barking in excitement. A female officer was posted inside the room so that Martha doesn't give the slip again. She stood there and smiled. They started playing monkey in the middle with the dog being the monkey.

Meantime Joseph made a phone call to his old friend Detective Shapiiro in Las Vegas. He explained the situation and was told to hang on to her and sit on her if necessary. Don't let her out of your signt for nothing in the world. They lfet Las Vegas and came in that evening to pick her up. He thanked Joseph for taking care of her. Detective Shapiro promised Martha she would go to the Mojave desert and live there permanently. They arrived at Detective Shapiro's home and settled in for the night.

C-H-A-P-T-E-R—26

The dog was a Beagle dog named Daisey. Robert told Daisey to take care of her and don't let her out of her sight. He made up the couch for her and she settled in for the night. When his wife got home from work she was surprised to see a little visitor. The dog took her instructions literally and laid on her stomach all night. She tried to get up once to to go the bathroom, but the dog growled and wouldn't move an inch. She called for Detective Shapiro and he lited the dog to let her up. His wife walked her to the bathroom and the dog slipped in to watch. When she came out she was tucked back into bed. Robert told his wife of the situation with the child. Martha managed to roll over and the dog moved over to face her. She put her chin on Martha's stomach so she couldn't move without being noticed. Martha went back to sleep after about fifteen minutes and slept the rest of the night.

In the morning Robert and his team met in his office for their Monday Morning meeting. He smiled and opened with the announcement that they have a new case. He put John in charge of it because Missing Persons seemed to be his specialty. They gathered in Rober't home for dinner that night for a dinner of Roasted turkey and Mashed Potatoes. Martha hd fun trying to help out with the cooking. She put a tablespoon of flour in the turkey bag and spread it around for the whole bag. She ahd to shake it up. That was fun for her. She asked about cranberry sauce for dessert. She was told to keep it in the refrigerator until ready to serve. Martha did most of the work and Robert's wife did most of the supervising. She didn't want it to turn into a long day for Martha. The dog layed in the kitchen and followed Martha's every move with her head and eyes. Eventually it started giving her the willies. At 5:00 p.m. Robert returned home with his team. He got out of his tie and put on a fresh shirt. The other members made themselves comfortable in front of the TV in the living room. The dinner was finally finished. Robert told Daisey to go lay down and her guard duty was over. She padded into the living room. Martha thanked Robert for sending the dog away. She was tired of being stared at. Introductions were made and they thanked the Lord for this good meal and talented wife for making it. Robert passed out drinks in coffee cups. Martha was the only one given a Christmas mug an everybody else got a mug with a dog on it. At 8:00 the group broke up so that Robert can get some sleep. His wife got stuck doing the dishes. Martha was put to bed early with Daisey right there taking up her post. At first Martha couldn't sleep, but she managed to talk to Daisey and then she fell asleep for the night. She awoke around seven the next morning. Robert cooked her a breakfast of scrambled eggs and toast.

By the time Robert got to the office John already had the mug at the lab for DNA analysis. About two hours later he got a return phone call from the lab that they had a hit. He got so excited he practically jumped through the door and hit Schapiro in the head. John got a call back from the lab that they had a hit on a missing child. Her real name was Wendy fromNew York. Schapiro called the New York police and was told that her aunt and uncle will be out on the niext flight to Las Vegas. They were told to sit on her and not to let her out of their sight for a minutes. Schapiro gave him the phone number of the station house. They called Schapiro back about an hour later and gave him the exact flight information. Schapiro decided to meet them at the airport so they don't get lost. Jon held up a big sign over his head with their names on it. This was to show them whom to hook up with. Wendy's aunt and uncle were excited about being in Las Vegas. John drove them to the Flamingo Hotel where Robert made reservations for them. John made a plan that Wendy would be reunited with them in the morning at 10:00 a.m. local time. They shouldn't leave the hotel until they returned with Wendy. They agreed to those conditions.

The next morning at precisely 10:00 Robert knocked on the door with Wendy at the front of the line.he two looked at her and knew right away she was their missing niece. They agreed to a DNA comparison test. That came back positive. They entered the room and sat at the table.

Robert asked; "Do you remember your aunt and uncle?"

Wendy said; "No sir. I have been alone in the world for two years at least. One day my parents just vanished, so that is what I did. I have no memory of being in New York."

Robert said: "We have to release you to your aunt and uncle. Their names are Helen and Joseph. He goes by the name of Joe."

Helen said: "We live upstate in new York in Dutchess County. You used to live in the city. We showed up at your mother's funeral and you were nowhere to be found."

Wendy said: "Oh. I have been traveling the United States ever since then. I have seen many things and met many people. I tried to walk west toward the Mojave Desert. I have always been fascinated by it."

Helen said: "Guess what my friend. You made it."

Robert said: "We will excuse ourselves now and leave you guys alone to get to knew each other. Helen and Joe thanked Robert profusely for his work in reuniting them together.

Robert said: "Oh. One more thing Helen. You have this room for a week, so you can stay until next Wednesday. Wednseday is the day of the least crowds." After Robert left Joe started looking through the book of possible itineraries. They picked out a few places to visit. She felt like a new person after a shower and a good night's sleep. They left Nevada and resettled in Dutchess County. September came around and Wendy was registered for 9th grade. She went for a required physical and discovered she had a hysterectomy. That explained her short stature and lack of body hair. She remembered the event. Somebody paid her to replace her as a patient. She would do anything for a warm bed and a hot meal and a shower. They all lived happily ever after.

Four years later they all returned to Las Vegas so Wendy could go to the university for a college education. Robert called a news conferenece to announce the founding of this missing child on the day of her being reunited with her relatives.